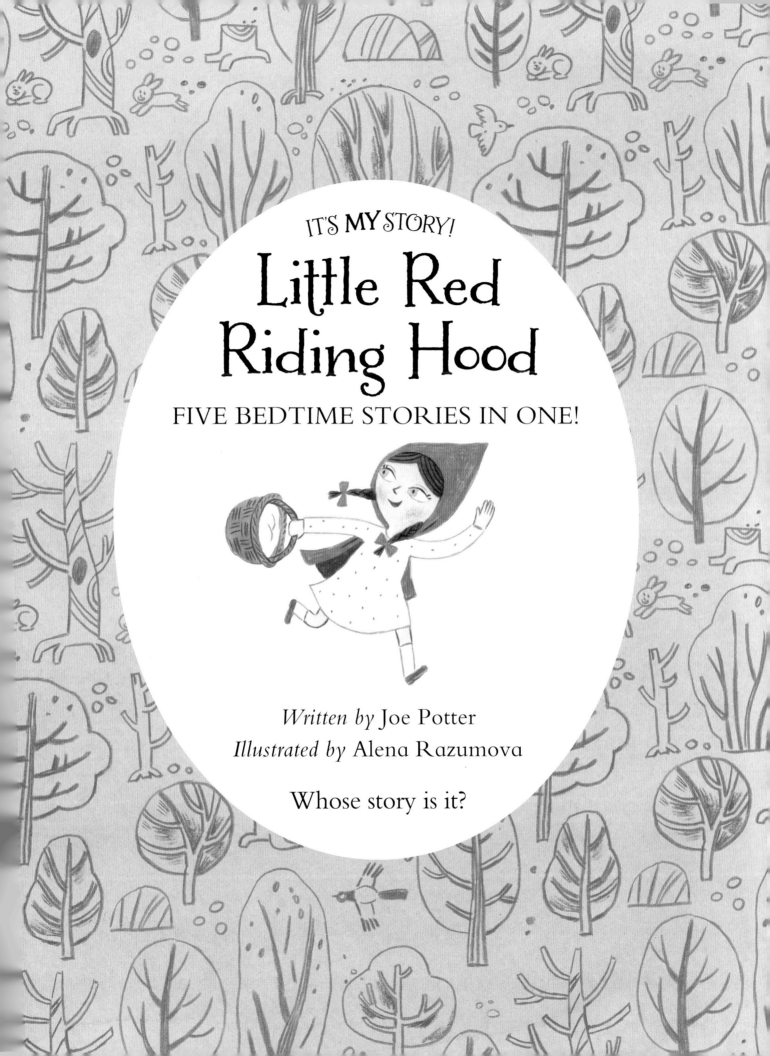

IT'S **MY** STORY!

Little Red Riding Hood

FIVE BEDTIME STORIES IN ONE!

Written by Joe Potter

Illustrated by Alena Razumova

Whose story is it?

CONTENTS

First published in the UK by iSeek Books
an imprint of iSeek Ltd.

Copyright © iSeek Ltd 2023
1A Stairbridge Court, Bolney Grange Business Park,
Haywards Heath, RH17 5PA, UK
12 Hatch Street Lower, Dublin, D02 R682, Ireland
iseekbooks.com

ISBN: 978-1-915458-83-4

Text by Joe Potter
Illustrated by Alena Razumova
Designed by Anton Poitier

Printed in China

This book is typeset in Bembo Infant

A CIP catalogue record for this book is available
from the British Library.

5 4 3 2 1

Once upon a time, I had a very strange day when I went to visit my granny. Want to know what happened? Well, let's begin with the story that you might have heard before and then I'll tell you myself about my day! Oh, by the way, everyone wants a look in, so they've told their story too – after me, of course!

Are you sitting comfortably?

WOODSMAN

WOLF

GRANNY

The Story You Might Have Heard

Once upon a time there was a little girl who lived near a forest with her mother. Everyone called her Little Red Riding Hood because of her bright red cloak. If ever you see a flash of red in the forest, it may well be Little Red Riding Hood.

One day Little Red Riding Hood realised she hadn't seen her granny in a very long time so she asked her mother if she could walk through the forest to visit her.

"That's a lovely idea," her mother said, "Granny must be very lonely in her cottage all by herself, so let's pack a basket full of delicious food to give her."

Before Little Red Riding Hood set off, her mother gave her a big kiss and a warning.

"Now remember, go straight to Granny's, don't dawdle in the forest and don't stray off the path."

"Don't worry, Mummy, I'll be careful." Little Red Riding Hood said and skipped out of the door.

"And don't talk to strangers!" her mother called after her.

It was a beautiful sunny day and by the time Little Red Riding Hood reached the forest she had quite forgotten her promise to her mother. Almost at once, she strayed off the path to chase a pretty butterfly into the bushes. Then, Little Red Riding Hood found some lovely flowers in a clearing and began to pick them.

But, deep in the forest, a pair of yellow eyes had caught sight of her bright red cloak. Little Red Riding Hood was so enjoying herself so much that she didn't notice a dark shadow looming over her.

"Hello little girl, what's your name and what are you doing here all alone?" came a deep voice from above her.

Little Red Riding Hood jumped up in surprise. Standing over her was an enormous grey wolf. Her mother had warned her not to talk to strangers but the wolf was smiling broadly and he looked very friendly.

"I'm Little Red Riding Hood and I'm on my way to see my granny who lives on the other side of the forest," she said. Little Red Riding Hood was just about to show the wolf the basket she and her mother had packed when she realised what the time was.

"I'm sorry Mr Wolf," she said, "I'm late to see my granny and I've got to get there before it's dark."

The wolf's smile broadened even further. When Little Red Riding Hood had skipped out of sight, he jumped into action.

He ran to Granny's cottage, taking a few short cuts so he could get there before Little Red Riding Hood. He crept up to the door and gave a knock with his furry paw. "Oh Granny, it's Little Red Riding Hood," the wolf said.

When Granny opened the door, she screamed and ran through the cottage, but the wolf caught her and gobbled her up! As soon as he'd swallowed her, there was a knock at the door.

"Hello Granny, it's me, Little Red Riding Hood!"

Quick as a cat, the wolf put on Granny's night clothes and jumped into her bed. "Come in, my dear. I'm afraid I'm not feeling very well and I'm upstairs in bed," said the wolf in a gruff voice.

"Granny, how strange you sound," said Red Riding Hood as she walked into the bedroom.

"It's just a little cold," croaked the wolf, and invited her to sit at the end of the bed.

Then Little Red Riding Hood noticed another very strange thing. "Granny, what big ears you have," she said.

"All the better to hear you with, my dear," the wolf replied.

Little Red Riding Hood was just about to open the basket when she noticed something else very odd about her granny. Her eyes seemed enormous and she didn't remember them being yellow.

"Granny, what big eyes you have," she said.

"All the better to see you with, my dear," the wolf replied.

Then Red Riding Hood noticed that her granny's teeth seemed to have grown.

"Granny, what big teeth you have," she said.

"All the better to eat you with, my dear!" growled the wolf and he leapt out of bed. Little Red Riding Hood realised it was the wolf and rushed downstairs. The wolf chased after her.

Little Red Riding Hood ran out of the door shouting "Help! Help! Wolf! Wolf! I think he's eaten my granny."

A woodsman, who knew Little Red Riding Hood's granny, was chopping wood nearby and he sprinted over with his axe. Just as the wolf was about to snap his jaws around Little Red Riding Hood, the woodsman grabbed him. They tussled and wrestled and, with a great squeeze from the woodsman, the wolf spat Granny out.

"Now off with you," the woodsman yelled, giving the wolf a final kick up the bum. The wolf ran into the forest.

"Thank goodness you were nearby Mr Woodsman," said Granny. "That wolf gobbled me up and he would have gobbled up my granddaughter too!"

"That's quite alright," said the woodsman, "but always remember, be careful around strangers, especially wolves."

"Thank you Mr Woodsman," Little Red Riding Hood said, and they all went into Granny's house and had a lovely cup of tea and cakes.

Little Red Riding Hood's Story

My name is Little Red Riding Hood. I'm eight years old so I'm not that little! I'm called Red Riding Hood because of my red cloak. It's very bright and I love it. Mummy said that you can always spot me in the forest when I wear my cloak. But now I know that may not always be the best thing!

A few days ago I realised I hadn't seen Granny for a long time, so I asked Mummy if I could walk through the forest to see her. Mummy said she thought that was a lovely idea as Granny was a bit lonely all on her own in her cottage. She phoned Granny to let her know I was coming, and we packed a basket full of goodies for her!

Mummy made me promise to go straight to Granny's, not to dawdle in the forest and not to stray off the path in the forest.

I told her not to worry, and then I skipped right out of the door (I like skipping!).

"And don't talk to strangers!" Mum said.

It was a beautiful sunny day. But, once I got to the forest, I forgot my promise to Mummy. A beautiful butterfly flew past and I really wanted to see it more closely, so I chased after it into the bushes. I'm really interested in butterflies and flowers and things. When I grow up I'd like to be a scientist who studies nature.

I couldn't keep up with the butterfly but I found some lovely flowers and wanted to look closely at them. I was so busy I didn't notice a huge shadow looming over me!

Then suddenly, someone with a deep voice said "Hello little girl, what are you doing out here all alone?"

I looked up and I saw a great big grey wolf! My mummy had told me not to talk to strangers, but he seemed quite nice.

"I'm Little Red Riding Hood and I'm on my way to see my granny who lives on the other side of the forest." I said. "My mummy packed a basket of food to give to her."

Maybe I can study this wolf? I thought. Suddenly I remembered my promise to Mummy.

"I'm so sorry, Mr Wolf, I'm late to see my granny and I've got to get there before it's dark." The wolf smiled at me and we waved goodbye to each other as I skipped to Granny's cottage.

I knocked on the door but Granny didn't answer.

"Hello Granny, it's me, Little Red Riding Hood!" I called.

"Come on in, my dear. I'm not feeling very well and I'm upstairs in bed," Granny replied in a strange voice.

I went upstairs and found Granny in bed. "How strange you sound. What's happened to your voice?" I asked.

"Oh nothing to worry about, my dear, just a bit of a cold," croaked Granny.

"You've brought me a basket of goodies. How kind. Come and sit with me, child."

I sat at the end of Granny's bed but as I got closer I noticed another very odd thing about Granny.

"Granny, what big ears you have," I said.

"All the better to hear you with, my dear," Granny replied.

Granny's eyes seemed ginormous behind her glasses and they looked yellow!

"Granny, what big eyes you have," I said.

"All the better to see you with, my dear," Granny replied.

Then I noticed that Granny's teeth were scarily big, not to mention her nose, which was grey and furry!

"Granny, what big teeth you have," I said.

"All the better to eat you with, my dear!" Granny growled.

And then Granny jumped out of bed! Of course, it wasn't Granny. It was the wolf wearing my Granny's clothes.

I rushed downstairs and out of the house shouting "Help! Help! Wolf! Wolf! I think he's eaten my granny."

Luckily, a woodsman heard my cries. Just as the wolf was about to gobble me up, the woodsman grabbed the wolf. They wrestled and tussled until the wolf spat out my poor granny.

Then the woodsman gave the wolf a sore bum with his boot and the wolf ran off into the forest.

"Thank goodness you were nearby Mr Woodsman," said Granny. "That wolf gobbled me up and he would have gobbled up my granddaughter too!"

The woodsman nodded and said: "Remember little girl, be careful around strangers, especially wolves."

I thanked the woodsman and we all went to Granny's for tea and cakes. I think I'd better listen to my mummy next time!

Granny's Story

Good day to you. My name is Iris. I live in a cottage near the forest. My granddaughter lives with her mother on the other side of the forest. Everyone calls her Little Red Riding Hood because her cloak, which I'm very proud of because I gave it to her for her birthday.

Would you like to hear a story about Little Red Riding Hood and myself? I warn you though, it's a bit scary and it involves a huge wolf who likes to gobble up grannies! You're brave enough aren't you? Alright then I'll tell you. Strap in, though, because it's a bit of a wild ride!

Last Tuesday, or was it Wednesday? Well, anyway, one day last week I received a telephone call from Little Red Riding Hood saying she was coming over and she had a surprise for me. I love surprises but nothing's as good as seeing your grandchildren. Immediately I set to sorting the house out, which was in a real mess! I cleaned it from top to bottom and side to side. Under the sofa, on top of the mantelpiece, around the cabinets and even up on the ceiling. I washed the dishes and swept the floor. I polished the surfaces until they gleamed, ready for Little Red Riding Hood's visit.

21

I was so excited when I heard a knock at the door. I could hear a little girl's voice saying, "Oh Granny, it's Little Red Riding Hood come to see you."

She sounded very strange, though, and I wondered if maybe she was ill? I opened the door and, to my horror, instead of Little Red Riding Hood, there was a huge, horrible wolf baring his great big teeth at me!

I span around completely terrified and ran off through the cottage. Oh how I screamed! Oh how I yelled! A big nasty wolf in my cottage! He'll make it all dirty again. I ran about shouting, "Help! Help! Help!" but no one was there to hear me.

Now I may be old but I still have a few tricks up my sleeve. As the wolf chased me round and round the living room, I grabbed the remote control and bonked him on the nose. The wolf fell back, clutching his hooter, and I ran upstairs to hide in my bedroom.

I shut the door and hid under my bed but the wolf sniffed me out. I heard him creeping up the stairs and then stop right outside my bedroom door.

"I know you're in there," he said, "my wolfy nose can smell grandmas a mile off."

"Go away," I shouted, but the wolf just laughed and bashed down the door!

The wolf ran in and pulled me out from under the bed! I've never struggled so much in my life. We jostled and wrestled and scrabbled and scrapped, but it was no good, the wolf was just too big and I'm only a little grandma, after all!

Then the wolf opened his huge jaws and gobbled me down in one. It's very dark inside a wolf's stomach. I tried to wriggle out but it seemed like I was swallowed for good. Just then I remembered Little Red Riding Hood. She would be coming though the door any minute and she didn't know about the wolf!

"Let me out of here this minute, you nasty old wolf!' I yelled. The wolf didn't answer but I could hear lots of muffled voices. I yelled again, "Little Red Riding Hood, Little Red Riding Hood, watch out for the wolf!" but she couldn't hear me either. And they say I'm deaf!

The next thing I knew I felt a big squeeze and I was shot out of the wolf's stomach. With a cough and a splat I landed on the ground. I was covered from head to foot in slime and grime. I looked up to see Mr Woodsman wrestling with the wolf and Little Red Riding Hood hiding behind him.

"Now off with you!" yelled Mr Woodsman and he gave the wolf a good kick up the bum. Off he shot into the forest whimpering, with his tail between his legs.

"Thank goodness you were nearby," I said to him, "That wolf gobbled me up and he would have gobbled up my granddaughter too!"

"That's quite alright," he said, and told her to be careful around strangers, especially wolves.

My granddaughter thanked Mr Woodsman very much and, because he'd been such a hero, I invited him in for tea and cakes.

The Wolf's Story

Well hello there! I am the wolf. Every story needs a villain you see and in this story the villain is me. But at the end of the day, I am a wolf and wolves are always looking for a tasty dinner – that's just the way it goes. So, let me tell you my story.

I was walking through the forest, minding my own business, when I saw a flash of red through the bushes. When I sneaked closer I was delighted to see a little girl in a red cloak picking flowers. What a delicious mouthful she would make, I thought. Yum, yum! And, believe me, I was hungry.

Very slowly I crept out of the bushes and I was just about to pounce when the little girl spotted me and jumped up. She looked a frightened so I put on my best smile and poshest voice and said,

"Hello little girl, what's your name and what are you doing here all alone?"

"I'm Little Red Riding Hood and I'm on my way to see my granny who lives on the other side of the forest. My mummy has given me a basket of food to give to her," explained the little girl.

So, there's a granny too, I thought. Just think of those crunchy old bones! Yum, yum, yum. I must go and visit Granny after I've gobbled this one up!

Suddenly, the little girl skipped off saying, "I'm sorry Mr Wolf, I'm late to see my granny and I've got to get there before it's dark."

Drat! I thought, I've missed my chance, but no matter because a plan was forming in my mind.

I ran off through the trees, taking a short cut to Granny's cottage. In a flash I was there. I trod lightly through the flower beds and tiptoed to the door. I gave a smart rap on the door and said in my best little girl's voice, "Granny, it's Little Red Riding Hood come to see you."

I waited patiently and, sure enough, Granny fell for my trick and came straight to the door. I opened my jaws wider than wide, wide enough to fit a granny inside. As soon as she saw me she screamed and ran off into the cottage, but you can't hide from Mr Wolf and, after a bit of a chase, and a surprisingly painful bonk on the nose from a remote control that Granny threw at me, I gobbled her up. Yum, yum!

One by one I put on Granny's bed clothes. First the flowery nightie, then the nightcap and finally the glasses. Looking out of the window I caught a flash of red coming down the path – it was Little Red Riding Hood swinging her basket. Just before she knocked to the door I jumped into Granny's bed and pulled the covers up to my nose.

Oh what a clever wolf I was! Oh what a wicked plan. Little Red Riding Hood would come bounding in thinking I was her granny and then when she least expected it I would jump up and gobble her down in one gulp!

I could hear Little Red Riding Hood calling, "Hello Granny, it's me, Little Red Riding Hood!'

I tried to make my voice sound old and croaky like Granny's, "Come in, my dear. I'm not feeling very well and I'm upstairs in bed."

I heard Little Red Riding Hood walking up the stairs. When she opened the bedroom door, she looked confused.

"Granny," she said, "how strange you sound. What's happened to your voice?"

"Oh nothing to worry about my dear, just a bit of a cold,"I said. "You've brought me some goodies – how kind, come and sit with me."

Little Red Riding Hood sat at the end of the bed but not close enough for me to gobble her up. Then she moved much closer to me saying, "Granny, what big ears you have."

"All the better to hear you with, my dear," I replied. I gave my best smile from ear to ear but still Little Red Riding Hood looked confused She leant in even closer and stared at me.

"Granny, what big eyes you have," she said.

"All the better to see you with, my dear," I replied.

I could have chomped her then, but it was too much fun! I flashed my bright white teeth and she gasped.

"Granny, what big teeth you have," she said.

"All the better to eat you with, my dear," I growled and leapt out of bed.

Little Red Riding Hood screamed and ran out of the bedroom. I chased her down the stairs and out into the front garden. She was shouting, "Help! Help! Wolf! Wolf! I think he's eaten my granny."

Then, suddenly, a woodsman came running over. I immediately recognized him as my old enemy. I was about to gobble up Little Red Riding Hood, when he grabbed hold of me and squeezed me so tight that out shot Granny!

Now, I don't like to tell you what happened next, but the woodsman kicked me up the bum and yelled, "Now off with you!"

I raced into the forest as fast as my legs would carry me. My bottom was very sore and my tail was quite bent. How could this have happened to me, Mr Wolf himself? Defeated by the old woodsman and a little girl in a red cloak. I think to be safe I'd better just stick to chasing rabbits from now on!

The Woodsman's Story

Hello, my name is Tom but everyone just calls me Mr Woodsman. Usually you'll see me in the forest with a big axe chopping up firewood but for every tree I cut down I always plant another one. Anyway, I thought I'd tell you about the time I went from just being a woodsman to being a hero.

Now, where shall I begin? Well I suppose it all started years ago when I found a wolf cub in the forest. He was all alone and he was shivering from the cold. I always look after the animals in the forest and, since he was only a very small wolf, I decided to take him home with me.

36

I fed him some milk and he perked right up. When I called him Mr Wolf he gave a happy howl and grinned at me. I could already see his little teeth but I thought if you could tame a dog surely you could tame a wolf? How very wrong I was.

To start with things were okay. The wolf cub drank from a bottle and slept and slept. But as he got older things changed. Two weeks later he was twice the size with sharp snapping jaws. He chased my chickens and frightened my cat. He ate up the sausages in my fridge and ripped up the mat.

And when he started to speak things got even worse. Oh, you didn't know wolves could speak? Well this one could! Wolves eat meat, but Mr Wolf was always talking about how he wanted to gobble anyone who wandered alone in the forest! I tried to explain that it was just plain wrong but he said he was a wolf and that's what wolves do.

By the time he was six months old, Mr Wolf could look after himself and I knew I couldn't keep him anymore. He was too big and too dangerous. I took him deep into the forest and found a cave for him to live in. I made him a bed of straw so he wouldn't get cold.

When I told him I was leaving Mr Wolf looked rather upset. "I'm sorry Mr Wolf but I just can't keep you anymore," I explained. Mr Wolf didn't look too sure about his new home, so I said "I'm sorry but you're a wolf and wolves are not meant to live among people."

When it got dark and the moon shone brightly, I heard a great howl. This made me feel a bit better because Mr Wolf only howled when he was happy. With any luck some other wolves might hear him and he could be with his own kind. After all, wolves are wild animals, not pets.

Years later, I was chopping wood in the forest when I heard a little girl yelling, "Help! Help! Wolf! Wolf! I think he's eaten my granny."

I knew it was Mr Wolf who was chasing the little girl. I stopped my chopping and ran over to help. I ran as I had never run in my life. I knew that wolves do what wolves do and it was my job to protect everyone who lived near the forest.

I saw the cottage belonging to an old lady I knew and, out of the door, burst a little girl wearing a red cloak. She was yelling and waving her arms. Mr Wolf came chasing after her, his jaws open wide. He was enormous now, bigger than me, with great big teeth and huge yellow eyes.

Just as Mr Wolf was about to gobble up the little girl I leapt in front of her and grabbed him. He growled and snapped but I didn't let go. With a huge squeeze I made him spit out Granny. The old lady looked very shaken up and she was covered in gunk!

"Now off with you!" I yelled and gave Mr Wolf a boot up the bum for good measure. He ran into the forest, whimpering. I don't know if he recognised me, and to tell you the truth, I felt a little sorry for him - after all he was only doing what wolves do.

"Thank goodness you were nearby, Mr Woodsman," Granny said to me, "That wolf gobbled me up and he would have gobbled up my granddaughter too!"

"That's quite alright," I said. "But remember, little girl, be careful around strangers, especially wolves."

"Thank you Mr Woodsman," she said, and invited me in for tea and cakes. I never told them I already knew Mr Wolf as a pup, but I promised I would always protect people from his snappy jaws!

THE END

And so now it's
time for bed!